Disney

A Cheerful Day

Written by
Guy Davis

Illustrated by
Dean Kleven

© Disney Enterprises, Inc.
Based on the "Winnie the Pooh" works, by A.A. Milne and E.H. Shepard.
All Rights Reserved.

Published by
Louis Weber, C.E.O.
Publications International, Ltd.
7373 North Cicero Avenue
Lincolnwood, Illinois 60712

www.pilbooks.com

Manufactured in China.

8 7 6 5 4 3 2 1

ISBN 1-4127-3027-9

"What a cheerful day it is," said Winnie the Pooh, humming happily.

But Pooh soon discovered that not everyone felt so cheerful. Eeyore didn't feel cheerful at all. In fact, Eeyore wouldn't come out of his house, or even turn around when Pooh called his name!

Pooh was worried. Eeyore always acted gloomy, but Pooh had never seen him *this* sad before! Pooh hurried over to Christopher Robin's house and explained the problem.

"You know what we must do?" said Christopher Robin. "We must throw Eeyore a party. And not just any party...an Appreciation Party!"

Christopher Robin quickly found
Piglet and Tigger and explained the
plan. "Let's each make a special
                    present for Eeyore,"
            he said.

"Then we'll meet at Eeyore's house," added Pooh.

"Parties are what tiggers like best!" cried Tigger.

After Piglet and Tigger left to make their gifts, Christopher Robin used ribbon to make a new bow for Eeyore's tail.

"Eeyore's bow is looking a bit worn," said Christopher Robin. "I'm sure he'll like having a new one to wear!"

Pooh watched as Christopher Robin wrapped Eeyore's gift.

"Think, think, think," said Pooh. "What would be the best gift of all to cheer Eeyore up? Why, honey, of course!" Pooh said. So Pooh went home to get his last pot of honey.

"Maybe I should try a little, just to make sure it's good and fresh," said Pooh.

"Mmmm, this smackerel is very tasty!" said Pooh, licking his honey-covered paw. "But perhaps I should try a bit more to be sure."

Before long, Pooh had eaten all of Eeyore's tasty present! "Maybe the last pot of honey isn't the best gift after all," said Pooh.

Piglet's idea was to make a fun, high-flying kite for Eeyore. Surely that would cheer him up!

So Piglet made the kite out of some sticks he'd found. But after Piglet put it together, it was too heavy. Piglet pulled and pulled, but the kite would not budge!

Tigger's gift for Eeyore wasn't going much better. Tigger wanted to give Eeyore a little bounce in his step, because bouncing was bound to make him feel cheerful!

As Tigger searched for an old spring he had seen, it started to rain. By the time Tigger found the rusty spring, there was no bounce left in it.

The friends all gathered at Eeyore's house. They explained to Eeyore that they were giving him an Appreciation Party!

"I was going to give you some honey," said Pooh, "but I ate it all."

"The kite I made is too heavy to move," added Piglet.

"And my spring," sighed Tigger, "doesn't have any bounce left."

Eeyore opened up Christopher Robin's gift and took out the new bow. Eeyore looked around at his friends and started to smile.

"Thanks for thinking of me, friends," said Eeyore, proudly trying on his new bow. "I really like it." The friends all cheered!

Eeyore didn't care about the empty honeypot, or the rusty spring, or the kite that wouldn't fly. He was just happy being with his friends.

And as the sun burst through the clouds, Eeyore thought to himself, "It really *is* a cheerful day."